Also by SE Bloom

The Secret Bloodline
Taken By The Slithering Horror

Table of Contents

TAKEN BY THE SLITHERING HORROR

SE Bloom

TAKEN BY THE SLITHERING HORROR

Digital Edition

Copyright © 2019 SE Bloom

DISCLAIMER

This is a work of fiction. Names, characters, places, and incidents either are the products of the author's imagination or are used fictitiously. Any resemblance to actual persons, living or dead, businesses, companies, events, or locales is entirely coincidental.

Use of terms is not meant to insult or otherwise upset any segment of the reader population. Terms such as 'Indian' rather than 'Native-American' are used because it is more appropriate to the setting, and not intended to be provocative.

This book is a work of erotic horror. The use of terms dealing with sex and sexual situations are a necessary component to books of this genre.

This book contains Adult Material and is intended for adult readers only.

1 ADVENTURE

REBECCA HEARD A MULTITUDE of Cicadas making their rustling sounds in the near distance. In the last few years, the climate in the Maricopa valley had completely changed, and the Cicadas had appeared from nowhere to bring a mournful note to the wilderness.

She looked over at her partner in crime. Eric was one of the few men Rebecca had ever found that could bring off that Blonde look, and still be masculine. Unfortunately, he was as self-centered and selfish as he was masculine.

They were scheduled to investigate a strange phenomenon that the local Salt River tribe had reported. Eric had a boner about checking out new and strange things, and the world was filling up with strange things that defied common sense.

The world had been getting weird for about five years now. This area used to be high desert, but now it was almost temperate terrain. It had a rainfall of over fifty inches a year, heavy cloud cover, and an odd ground cover that included grasses, palm trees, cacti, and other plants that were possibly transplanted from local residents gone wild, and a sprinkle of plants and saplings of types that nobody had ever seen before.

They were on the porch of Eric's wilderness house, a sort of cabin near the reservation that he maintained from which to mount his investigations. Rebecca had strung along with this current excursion, principally because she had happened to be drinking coffee in the same coffee shop where the young Indian had met Eric to spill the beans about the current strange thing.

"Are you ready to go visit a cave?" Eric asked. "It really sounds like there is something to this report."

"I thought you would never finish packing for the trip," Rebecca quipped. "For someone who claims to be a man on a mission, you sure take your time."

An expression that mixed anger, surprise, and something approaching a brief twinge of panic visited his face for a second before he succumbed to a standard sarcastic expression. "It is hard to be sure to include the appropriate equipment for an investigation when you don't know what you are investigating," he declared, "It is not like you girls. I did not spend time figuring out the best outfit to wear."

Rebecca gave Eric a smiling smirk, and she regained her feet from her previous perch on the porch swing. The backpack she had packed for the trip was at her feet, and in a second, she had positioned in on her shoulder. Eric's pickup awaited them in the driveway.

They put their belongings in the back of the pickup and found their seats in the cab of the vehicle. As all girls must, the first thing that Rebecca did was to adjust the visor to a position where she could inspect her head and hair through the mirror attached.

She was finally satisfied that her long straight black hair and almost emerald green eyes were just as fetching as always. Rebecca flipped the visor back up and leaned back in her seat for the long ride ahead. Eric glanced over at her with a sneeringly amused grin, and then he started the engine of the overdone vehicle for the trip.

She returned his glance with a small degree of disgust, an emotion that she frequently dispensed to those who were patently unfair in their personal judgments. His smirk changed to a more serious and sober countenance as he brought the vehicle up to cruising speed, and pointed it toward the reservation.

The soul of fairness herself, Rebecca mentally reflected that while the man was an asshole, he did have some mitigating qualities. He was honestly interested in the modern mysteries that the world found to be all around humanity these days. While Eric had been condescending to her, he had never actually lied to her about anything. Maybe he could be converted to human after someone rearranged his face with a shovel.

Twenty minutes later, the couple was about to leave the well-defined roadways of the Phoenix Metro area in favor of the reservation roadways. As Eric diverted the vehicle onto the two-lane paved road that led onto the reservation, Rebecca found herself covertly examining the man driving the vehicle.

Eric was the proud possessor of short blonde hair, light blue eyes, and those rugged good looks that are never tested in action in the metrosexual world that city living subjected all of its male citizens to live in. Rebecca preferred the rugged good looks that could only be found on the visiting cowhands in a city such as this, but she had to admit that Eric was easy on the eyes.

She grew up in a part of the country where there were a lot of farmers with the looks that struggling with the land created. She had moved here from Arkansas about ten years ago, and every day, she wondered if she had made a mistake. She could have found a farmer, or what they call ranchers out here, and she thought that it might have made her happy.

The thought of moving back to Arkansas had become almost impossible in the last five years, ever since the world had become strange. Now she wasn't even sure that she would recognize her old neighborhoods. Unknown creatures were regularly reported in the woods back there, and more than one of her old friends had gone missing, never to be heard of again.

"Jimmy Two-Feathers said to meet him at the escarpment overseeing the cave," Eric remarked. "He said that he would show us the situation, but that he would not go anywhere near the cave. He sounded sincerely afraid of that place."

Eric indicated the Garmin affixed to the windshield. "We should be at the meeting place in about 15 minutes, according to Garmy here," he said. Just as he said that he diverted the truck off the pavement and onto a gravel road leading toward some small rocky hills.

2 PREPARATION

THEY ROLLED ALONG THE gravel road for about five minutes toward one of the rocky outcroppings in the area. That was just long enough for the regular crunching sound of the gravel beneath the tires to lull her into a state bordering on nodding off.

They actually left the gravel at the final stage in the journey in favor of the stone and dirty sand of the outcropping itself. There was an old jeep sitting at the highest point available. It looked as though it only had a fifty percent chance of being drivable.

Eric pulled their pickup truck alongside the old Jeep and brought it to a halt. Rebecca and Eric got out and began to walk over to the overly excited Indian man waiting for them. As soon as she reached the old Jeep, the Indian leaned forward to vigorously shake her hand and declared his name to be Jimmy. From the look on his face, she thought that he felt the number of white women he had bedded might be at least one short of optimal.

Jimmy handed a set of old binoculars to Eric and waved in the direction of the dark mouth of the cave that the couple can now see in the mountainous rock face ahead of them. "There have been a lot of animals going into the cave recently," Jimmy said, "but nobody has seen any of them come back out."

"I think that a few people may have gone in there as well," he continued, "At least, a few tribe members that were in this area have gone missing recently."

"So, what do you think is in there?" Derek asked Jimmy. "Do you think that there is some sort of creature in there or some kind of force?"

"I don't know what to think of it," Jimmy said, "All I know is it scares the hell out of me, and I don't plan on going in there ever!"

"Well, the more, the merrier," Eric said, "but I do understand not wanting to walk into the unknown. Well, I guess that the only thing left is to get you paid, and then Rebecca and I can go find out what is going on."

Jimmy looked eager about the paying part. Chances are he intended for his friends and him to find a little liquid courage and tuck themselves into one of the dilapidated shacks that the Pima tribe called their homes for a long-lost weekend of debauchery.

Eric handed Jimmy five one-hundred dollar bills. "I will be taking the binoculars on my trip in as part of the deal," Eric said. "I will return them to you after we have checked things out."

Jimmy nodded his agreement and got into his old Jeep for the short ride to the liquor store. He started the process of cranking the old wreck, every turn of the starter sounding as though it might be the last. After several long seconds, the old engine finally caught, and Jimmy pulled out and away from his personal nightmare.

"Well, there goes our last chance at a personal Sherpa for this trip," Eric joked. "This puts a different spin on the idea of an Indian Brave to what we were taught in school." He handed the binoculars to Rebecca and turned around to paw through his bag to sort out what he wanted to carry with him into the cave.

3 THE PLANNING

REBECCA DIDN'T HAVE anything that she planned to take into the cave, depending on Eric's forethought to produce whatever she might need in there. Having nothing better to do, she turned toward the cave and started inspecting the terrain, and the path down to the mouth.

Just as she was about to conclude her inspection of the site, she caught a glimpse of movement just to the right of where she had focused the binoculars. Panning slightly more right, she saw a big black bear wandering toward the entrance. As she watched, the bear reached the cave mouth and disappeared into the blackness within the cave.

She felt a massive disquiet at the thought of following such a big predator into the unknown, and she turned toward Eric to tell him about the bear. He was in the process of taking the 30-30 that had been in the rack behind Rebecca's head on the trip out here out and checking the magazine for readiness.

"I just saw a bear going into that cave," she commented. "I would ordinarily ask you if you really want to take a gun into a cave visit, but I have to admit that I am a little happy that you thought to bring one."

"I usually try to arm myself to some degree out in the wild," Eric replied. "You never know what you will encounter. Since I don't want to die, I think that I will be taking it with me."

"Do you think that we should wait a while," she asked, "and give the bear a chance to leave before we go in?"

He handed her a flashlight, and one of those lanterns with LED lights in it that simplified overall lighting in dark places. He zipped up the gym bag that contained his equipment and slung the bag on his shoulder.

"We could wait for days for him to come back out," Eric mused. "That is one reason I brought the gun. If we see him, don't worry. We will give him a lot of space."

He pulled the bolt back to load the first bullet in the chamber, held the rifle tightly at the ready, and grinned a smug grin at her. Rebecca had to admit to herself that having an armed man as an escort into the unknown was slightly reassuring. She was starting to wish that she had the wisdom to bring at least a handgun of her own to this party.

He started to walk slowly toward their destination. She began to follow reluctantly behind him, reflecting that it was probably more dangerous to back out and stay out here in the wild than it was to follow the man with the gun.

They walked slowly toward the cave, with Rebecca trailing Eric by three paces, and wondering why she didn't go to the mall instead of coming along on this suicidal adventure. All too soon, they reached the cave.

4 THE CAVE

ERIC'S KNUCKLES TURNED white from the tension with which he was grasping the rifle. He fished at his belt for the flashlight that he had previously proudly dubbed a "torch," and aimed it into the cave's darkness, and turned it on.

The beam cut the darkness ahead, and they could see into the cave for about three hundred feet. It appeared that the cave went straight back for that distance, and then it turned to the right, obscuring the rest of the journey behind the rock of the walls.

"Well, at least the bear is nowhere in sight," Eric sighed. "Hopefully, he found his way out of there by some unknown back door. I am not confident that my rifle could bring him down fast enough to be safe."

"Now you tell me that you have doubts!" Rebecca protested. "I sure hope that I can run faster than you can if we see the bear. I know that I will try like hell!"

They hesitated for a few more moments. Eric checked his possessions once more while trying to rally a semblance of his former self-confidence. When it was obvious that he was running out of things to delay him further, Rebecca decided to engage him in a little pertinent conversation, just to delay the inevitable.

"So what is your theory about how all of this ties together?" Rebecca asked. "Do you have any idea about how all these strange events around the world are related to each other?"

Eric assumed a thoughtful demeanor, happy to have something to do besides rushing headlong into the unknown at that moment. He turned to face her completely and prepared to deliver his best conspiracy of the unknown.

"When it all started, people were coming up with all manner of ridiculous ideas about what was going on," he began. "There were the End of the Worlders, the alien invasion nuts, the strange space crazies, the Consensus of the Id cults, and last but not least, the return of the gods' sects. Out of all of them, the best ones are the alien invasion, the Consensus of the Id, and the return of the gods. I don't know which one is the true case, or if it is some sort of mixture of them. I tend to favor the return of the gods, in either the Anunnaki or even the Old Ones flavors, but I do not think there is any way of knowing the truth. That is why we are here, to look for the answers."

"What kind of a god would make the world so insane?" Rebecca protested. "Even the old Greek gods did things that made sense, even if they were selfish."

"That is why I tend to think that they are more like the Cthulhu Mythos gods that HP Lovecraft wrote about," Eric reflected. "They would always drive men insane, and nothing they did made any sense, except that they tended to destroy things. There has been some speculation in recent years that HP did not actually invent them, just rewrote real deities that really existed, and they so affected life on earth that some sort of memory of them were embedded in the very genes of life on earth. We have them as Archetypes in our minds, and gods such as Tiamat and the other chaos gods were nothing but dim memories of them."

"That idea gives me the shivers," Rebecca admitted. Indeed, she felt fear goose bumps on the skin of her legs and arms. Nothing sounded better than to go home and feed the cat.

They took a few more moments to pat down their various pockets and packages to make sure that they were ready to proceed. Eric took a deep breath and stepped a single step inside the cave.

"Come on," he said. "Let's get this thing going."

Rebecca felt some temerity as she followed him on his path into darkness. Eric turned on one of the lanterns that they brought with them, and the couple intently inspected their surroundings.

The first thing that struck them was the smell. There was a strong musky odor in the air, a smell that reminded Rebecca of old mushrooms. The second thing they noticed was the absolute lack of any other life in sight. There were no bats such as you would suspect in an inviting cave of this sort.

There were no insects or other bugs crawling on the rocks, and no snakes or other reptiles or amphibians were lounging on the rocks. The dark coolness of a cave should have been a beacon to these creatures, but none of them were within sight.

They advanced slowly deeper into the cave, using their flashlights to inspect the rocky walls and floor of the cave as they advanced. There was no events or objects to reassure them of their safety, but there was also none to tell them of danger.

When they reached the bend in the cave that would take them right, they had become used to the environment and proceeded into the section with more confidence. The smell of mushrooms was slightly more intense, as one would expect. There had been no noises that might be wildlife or other dangers.

About a hundred feet along the new route, the cave took a left bend. When they reached that bend and discovered what it contained, it brought them to an abrupt halt.

Before them was a huge pile of gleaming bone, a hill of ribs and skulls and small bones reaching up to a height of about ten feet. They could see the occasional bit of animal hide, and here and there were small scraps of the meat still attached to the bones.

"What the hell?" Rebecca exclaimed. "I think that we should get out of here!"

"It is just a pile of bones," Eric mused. "I know it looks ominous, but maybe it is just a strange sort of animal graveyard.

Animal graveyards had been noted for centuries, where one species or another had picked a particular place for the old and infirm to go to when they were about to die. The problem with that idea was that there were dozens of species in this heap of bones. They would not have picked the same place to die, would they?

"That's bullshit," Rebecca protested. "This is nothing natural. There are at least a dozen species here that I can identify, and something killed them."

Just as she was about to expand on her point, she saw in the middle of the pile, a human skull that brought her fear to the front. She grabbed Eric's arm, pulling him to the nearest vantage to the skull, and simply pointed.

She was about to exclaim, "Let's get the fuck out of here" and drag Eric out of the cave by force if necessary when suddenly, a vast sense of calm washed over her. She knew that it could not be a natural reaction, but she was suddenly feeling an imperative to continue deeper into the cave.

She looked at Eric and saw that he too seemed to be making the same transition from fright to the impulse to push on. At some deep level of her mind, her voice was screaming to her to run. Something else in her mind forced her to ignore that small scream.

Eric grabbed her hand, and said, "Come on! Let's see what is further in."

She found herself willingly led further into the cave, even though she knew that something was tampering with her natural caution. They continued into the passage, hand in hand, looking about themselves with both fear and an unnatural eagerness.

The cave began to incline downward as they traveled, making it easier to plod ahead, and taking them deeper into the bowels of the earth. The musty smell was getting stronger as they went deeper into the cavern. It struck Rebecca for the first time that it smelled just like sperm smells when the blowjob ends with a swallow.

It was terrifying some part of her mind that she was willingly going deeper into this dangerous place. She was now certain that something other than herself was directing her into this great chasm.

5 THE COMPULSION

THEY MUST HAVE WALKED for more than a quarter of a mile, maybe half a mile, when they heard the unmistakable sound of water running over a waterfall of some kind. There was just that hint of the water scent in the air that confirmed that they were near water. There also was a light foggy haze covering the cave floor on which they were walking.

A little later, the cave took another sharp turn, and the two of them caught their first sight of the waterfall that the sound had advertised. It was an eerie sight to see, with the fog moving around the cave floor in waves, and with the prismatic effect of the lantern-light, as the only source of illumination, on the falling water making almost a rainbow effect.

Here the mushroom smell was the most potent that Rebecca had yet experienced. The musk mixed with the smell of the waterfall, and the fog and the unusual lighting produced a surreal experience for the couple.

It was obvious from the expressions on Eric's face that he was having the same compulsion as she to remain in the cave, and wanted just as desperately to leave. Unfortunately, he was no longer in control.

That urge to move deeper into the cave was no longer pushing them on further into the cavern. Apparently, the waterfall was supposed to be their destination.

Rebecca took the opportunity to sit down on a rocky promi-
nence, and Eric found a place nearby to do the same thing. It felt
much better to take a load off her feet, even if some part of her
mind was still screaming.

"Are you still feeling a compulsion to stay here instead of
leaving the cave?" Rebecca asked. "I think some large part of me
is terrified, and something has a hold on my mind, forcing me to
stay, and making me calm in the front part of my head, while the
back screams."

"I could not have said it better myself," Eric admitted. "I
know that this has got out of control, and I have been trying to
force my legs to take me back out, but they will not obey me.
There is something here that can override our bodies. Something
we have never seen before."

It occurred to Rebecca that the conversation they were having was essentially a form of resistance to the compulsion, whatever it was. Simultaneously with that thought, she noticed a significant increase in the smell of ripe mushrooms, her mind started feeling blurry, and she felt a momentary dizziness.

She suddenly felt hot. She felt her skin flush, and every part
of her felt like it gained a few degrees of temperature. It was the
sort of thing that she imagined that post-menstrual symptoms
might feel like, only there was a wetness in her pussy that suggested that she was not sexually reduced in any way.

In her extremity, she looked over at Eric, who seemed to
be going through something similar to her own trials. He was
pulling off his shirt and his vest, which she thought was a good
idea if they wanted to mitigate this seeming heat-bath. She began
tugging at her own blouse when she lost track of herself.

The world became hazy for a minute. The smell of the musk was almost a physical thing, like a tiny seed actually resident in her nose. Her sense of time washed away, there must have been a period of time where she was gone into some sort of mental coma.

She awoke to the sensation of her kissing Eric deeply, as she struggled to remove his pants. He was returning the kiss and had just succeeded in removing her shorts. Her blouse was already discarded.

Finally, all of their clothes were gone, and she clutched him closely as she dragged him down to the floor. He entered her immediately, and just the feeling of his cock entering her forced her first orgasm. She throbbed and clutched, bucking beneath him as he thrust as deeply into her as he could.

That first climax became a continuous orgasm. The muscles of her pussy were having endless spasms, and long before he spurted his semen deep inside of her, she felt the expanding wet spot beneath her ass, where her pussy juices were being pulled out by each movement of his penis into and out of her body.

The length of time that transpired before he ejaculated might have been a source of embarrassment for a man in other circumstances, but totally forgivable given the urgency that both of them felt. No sooner had he spurted his cum deep into her than she freed herself from her position beneath him, rolled him over on his back, and reached for his still rigid cock.

She licked his cock with her tongue, savoring the taste of his semen and her pussy juices still on its skin. As soon as the taste diminished, she took the head of the organ into her mouth and began to give him a deep and devoted blowjob.

She slid her tongue over the head of his penis each time it was positioned where her tongue could find it, and reverently encased his shaft with her mouth. She had never been as turned on, as in heat, as she was here in this cave. At this moment, she knew that it was fate or destiny for her to be penetrated in every way by cocks, and it would be beyond her control to ever deny the right of any man to be serviced by her body in the future.

Eric began to thrust upward into her mouth more urgently, and when he finally spurted a large load into her mouth, she received it with a lust she had never felt before, and she swallowed all of it as soon as it was given to her waiting throat.

There was another shift in the status of the world at this point. The musk of the cave combined with the taste of the musky semen to attain an even more potent level. She felt dizzy, and her eyesight blurred once more before she once again lost time.

When she came to herself once more, she was on top of the man, riding him in cowgirl position. She barely let him remove his shaft in any amount, sitting with it embedded as deeply as she could make it.

Instead of moving up and down on the shaft, she was rocking her cunt forward and backward. The muscles of her pussy were out of control, squeezing and clutching his organ in the midst of endless orgasms.

He was holding her by the waist with one hand cupping her willing ass, thrusting upward into her cunt. This went on for longer than the first fuck, but all too soon, she felt him cum into her pussy again.

She collapsed down against his chest, with his shaft still inside her. Her cunt was continuing to spasm with orgasms, which was making his cock remain hard inside her.

She must have lost more time because the next thing she was aware of was Eric talking. "It must be pheromones," he said.

"What?" she asked. "What are you saying?"

"The fact that our urge to fuck is so far out of control," he began, "suggests that this cave is full of pheromones, driving us to copulate. Nothing else makes sense."

"I just thought that you thought I was hot," Rebecca returned, almost joking. "If there are pheromones here doing this to us, where did they come from?"

There are certain species that mimic the pheromones of other species in order to influence them," he explained. "Usually it is a way to make them pacified so that they can easily hunt and kill the prey, but sometimes it is used to get other species to do things for you because they accept them as part of their social structure. Raise your young for you. Things like that."

"Yeah, but what would do that to a human?" she asked. "I have never heard of anything that did that to people."

"What if the concept of the Cthonic gods that HP Lovecraft wrote about was some kind of racial memory of real entities?" speculated Eric. "He did not give us a sound basis for what they could do, but what if they existed, and they could influence people to do things, or just go crazy. Maybe they really existed, and the way they got into people's head was with pheromones and other chemicals. Maybe they also emitted hallucinogens to affect people's minds. Maybe they still exist and have been hiding for thousands of years, but now they are back."

"If that is really what is happening," she said, "then we need to get out of here!"

"Do you feel like you can leave?" he asked. "I have been trying to get my body to agree to leave, but I cannot make it get up and walk out."

Rebecca realized that he was right. She felt fear, and the need to flee, but it was behind some kind of mental curtain. Her mind was telling her that she was safely where she was supposed to be, and her body refused to obey the fear.

She realized that the influence of the pheromones must have been diminished for a short time since they had an opportunity to talk instead of suffering from a maddened lust for each other. She doubted that it would last very long. If they could not force themselves out of the cave before it returned, she doubted that they would ever escape.

One way she could gauge the level of influence on her was to compare what she was feeling with what was normal for her. She had never seen Eric as very sexually attractive, even if he was relatively handsome.

Right now, she was seeing him the way she normally did. It was inconceivable that they had just spent a large amount of time virtually raping each other. He was a conversation over coffee material, not breakfast in bed material.

"Let us get to our feet and try to work up the will to get out of here," Rebecca suggested. "I don't know how long we have before the compulsion takes over again, and I don't think that we will break free if it happens again."

"I think that you are probably right," Eric replied. "Let's get up and try to go."

6 CAPTIVE

HAVING AGREED TO THE only reasonable course of action, they struggled to their feet, with only the usual protests of overused muscles to stop them. They were still very naked, with their belongings scattered over an area spanning about fifty feet. Most of the light they were seeing by was coming from one of the electric lanterns, lying on its side about ten feet away.

"Grab your clothes, and let's go!" Rebecca demanded urgently. She turned her own attention to finding and retrieving her clothes. She was anxious to get away because she doubted that they had long to act.

The first item she reached was her bra, and as she turned to place it in her bag, the smell of the musk in the air intensified. She felt dizzy again, and the world she saw around her seemed to change. Her vision seemed to shift and alter, like seeing a light behind a pane of glass with water running over it.

She turned to see Eric. He was standing nearby, looking as disoriented as she felt. "He hasn't done anything to get ready to leave," she thought, as the world around her seemed to darken. The last thing she thought before consciousness left her was, "Not again."

The next thing she felt was being penetrated from behind by the man. His rigid cock was docked deeply within her willing cunt. His left hand was cupping her sensitive tits, and his fingers were playing with her hardened nipples. His right hand was at her waist, pulling her soft body back and forth on his hard shaft.

She noted with some small rational part of her mind that they were standing close to the rocky outcropping, and she was leaning over the rock, and pushing her ass backward with every thrust of his cock. Her orgasms were continuous again, and for the first time, she suspected that her body would never be content to have a day in the future when it was not being taken and fucked forcefully. For the first time, she realized that she was addicted to unlimited sex, an addiction that she would never be able to defeat.

Eric took his left hand off her tits and put it on the left side of her waist, to penetrate her even more forcibly than he had been penetrating her before. His thrusts had become far more urgent, even animalistic, and his rigid cock felt as if it had grown thicker and longer as it plunged in and out of her. She realized that she was moaning in heat and desire with every stroke of his member into her body.

The fucking went on and on, every thrust seeming to be harder and deeper. Rebecca was nothing but a receptacle for sensation now, the feeling of his dick-head moving in and out of her was the focus of her entire mind. Her pussy would attempt to hold his member by clamping down the muscles each time he started to withdraw.

Finally, he exploded inside her cunt with the largest load that he had delivered yet, and it was the largest load she had ever felt. The spasms of her orgasm made the sensation so intense that she felt her consciousness fading away once more.

7 THE CREATURE

REBECCA OPENED HER eyes. The pale light from the up-turned lantern, and the cold mist of the cave floor greeted her. She found herself slumped against the rock outcropping that she had formerly leaned against, almost where she had been in her last memory.

She looked over her shoulder to find Eric slumped in a similar fashion about three feet away. He opened his eyes and stared at her with a look of despair. The look on his face matched exactly the way she felt, and she knew that the way he had a dullness to his usually bright blue eyes also must be reflected in her own emerald green eyes.

"We cannot leave, can we?" he said in a dull and plaintiff voice.

"I don't think so," she replied. "I think that we have been here too long, and whatever creature is here has completely trapped us."

They had run out of things to say with that brief exchange. There was nowhere they could go, and any attempt to escape would be met by the loss of their free will. They were trapped here, in the control of whatever evil thing lived here, and there was nothing they could do about it.

There is a strange comfort in depression when it occurs to the depressed person that they had no control over their destinies. When you cannot make your life better, there are no requirements for you.

Rebecca was feeling that paradoxical feeling now. She had no power to leave this place, and she knew it. There was nothing left to do except wait to see what would happen next. She was giving up. Whatever she would live through in the coming hours, or if she would die, was no longer up to her, but to whatever power had control of her.

Yes, she was almost comfortable now. She should just think of her situation for what it was. She was now a slave to an unknown master, a master that could play her like a puppet whenever he wished, and there was nothing she could do about it.

The two of them stared dully at each other for long moments. They were both giving up hope, and each of them could read that in the other one. Rebecca thought that it was especially hard on Eric. Being controlled by someone else is even harder for men than it was for women.

Even in her current depressive state, that was almost funny. Men had always been controlled by their women, but most of them never knew that because the women learned how to do it subtly. Women had also made a point of claiming to be submissive to their men, pulling their strings all the while.

The moment of mental humor passed, and both of them were lost in their misery for an unknown amount of time before something happened that brought them back to their senses. There was a noise in the back of the chamber that brought them to their feet. For the moment, they had the volition to flee from possible danger.

From the thickest mists on the floor, approximately in the center of the open flooring before them, a stalk of some living material rose out of the mists. On the top end of the stalk, there was an eye, a gigantic eye that looked at them in a dispassionate and cold appraisal.

The sight of this alien eye was mind shattering for Rebecca. There was nothing about this sight that her mind could accept as real, and she wondered if she had finally descended into insanity.

For an instant, they were free of any compulsion to stay, and they turned to run away from this monstrosity. As Rebecca started to run, two tentacles (she did not know how else to describe them) rose from the mists. One of these tentacles wrapped around one of her legs, and then the second one found an equivalent grip on the other leg.

The tentacles were jet black, huge, with some suction cups located along their bottom sides, and strong beyond anything that she had ever experienced. She almost fell, but the tentacles held her legs in place, so that she could not fall, but had to remain where she was, on her feet.

She turned to plead with Eric to free her. He also was held by tentacles just like the ones that held her. He was struggling helplessly, but he had no chance of getting free.

Knowing that Eric was just as trapped as she was brought a level of terror to her that she had never felt before. He was the only hope she had hoarded for escape, and if he was trapped, she could not count on his help. There was truly no hope.

Rebecca and Eric were startled into a state of shocked fear when there was a sudden roar from the throat of the cave in the shadows beyond the range of the lanterns. One of the shadows separated from the others, and a terrifying and strange creature emerged.

There were parts of many different animals in whatever this thing was. Rebecca could see the faces of several people, probably the missing Indians, and there was parts of a wolf, a horse, and a mountain lion, all of which was installed within the body of a black bear. She wondered dully if it was the same black bear that they saw wander into the cave before them.

The thing saw them and roared, rushing toward the pair. It ignored Rebecca, but it went directly to Eric. He screamed as the teeth of the bear, and those of the wolf clamped down on his shoulder and his neck.

Rebecca screamed, and her screams were echoed by the screams from the faces of the people in the creature. The look of horror on their faces mirrored the look that must be on her face. As the blood began to spurt, and the creature secured its grip on Eric's limp body, the tentacles holding him retracted back into the mist.

The creature began dragging the body further back into the cave. In a moment, it was out of sight. From far away, Rebecca started hearing eating sounds, which went on for a long time. The fear and loathing were too intense, and she felt her consciousness fade away once more.

8 TENTACLES

SHE FELT SOMETHING muscular and smooth tracing patterns on her naked body, and she felt herself being held in place on the legs and around her waist. Every touch on her skin resulted in a body shaking orgasm, building to unbearable intensity.

Her cunt was dripping with secretions, aroused and ready to be filled. The musk in the air was no longer a smell. It was as though it was smoky tendrils reaching down into her lungs, and saturating all her cells.

She opened her eyes to discover that she still stood in the cave in front of the waterfall. The eye was back, focused on her with dispassionate intensity. The cave floor had different kinds of tentacles emerging from the mists in several places.

She wanted to scream. She wanted to die. She wanted to remember who she was, and how she got there. It was getting very hard to think. Her body was calling all the shots now, and it was carrying her along to a very dark destiny.

Two tendrils that resembled fronds of some wide leaved plant came out of the mist and fastened themselves to her sensitive nipples, gently massaging them and contributing yet another layer to her overwhelming explosive orgasms. Another tentacle rose up to her face. She had just enough time to goggle at the resemblance of the tip of the tentacle to the head of a man's penis before it forced its way into her mouth and began the age-old rhythm of oral sex.

Almost as soon as it began, warm musky liquid started pulsing out of the tentacle. It tasted like cum, but it also tasted like something resembling clam chowder. Her body sucked the strange semen in as fast as it spurted out.

She heard strange sounds, something rhythmic like a chant in the distance, and a sound that was similar to a harmonic sound produced by some sort of echo of unearthly sounds. The feeder in her mouth pulsed an extremely large load into her mouth, swelling physically to exude the cum into her mouth. It collapsed to its smallest size after the pulse and withdrew itself.

She saw something then at her feet that was not the expected tentacles. There was something there, which resembled a cylindrical cone made of a flesh substance. As she watched, it moved, elongating itself nearly to double its former length.

She noticed with terrified fascination that the tip of it had a slit in the same way that the protuberance that had fed her the cum-food had been slit. Even in the depths of her painful ecstasy, she was terrified of what that thing being there meant.

As she fearfully watched the thing, it slowly increased in size and elongated still more, until it was almost all the way up her legs, and about six inches in diameter. It actually bumped into her leg then, and the climax she felt as it made contact almost made her faint again.

She tried to lunge away from the strange thing in front of her, only to feel the tentacles around her legs and waist tighten to hold her firmly in place. Not even able to act on this one small attempt at independent self-preservation, the pervasive depression that she felt below the ecstasy became even more overwhelming.

The protruding arm of whatever monster lived within the floor of the cave extended the tip of itself out and toward her like it was budding off the main trunk of the organ. It was perhaps two inches in diameter.

It came on, closer and closer to her cunt, until it finally made contact with the lips of her vagina. An explosive series of orgasmic shocks ran through her body. The creature was at the gates of her body, which it held in a position that exposed her sex to any action it wanted to commit. She could not stop it.

The head of the thing began to force its way into her dripping cunt. She moaned harshly, and her body acted of its own accord to buck forward, further impaling her on its muscular shaft.

She felt the head of the shaft swell to a size so large that she could barely endure it, and it slowly forced its way as far into her as it could go without tearing out her organs. It then began to grow the thickness of the inserted shaft to barely fit within her now stretched pussy.

The organ then began elongating and contracting to make its way deeper in and out of her cunt, with every stroke doubling the intensity of her continuous orgasms. It moved with such force that she was picked up off the ground and returned with every stroke.

She was feeling more pain than she had ever imagined possible, and more pleasure than she could endure. It was so intense that she felt her mind wash away each time it pushed its way deeper inside of her.

Only a tiny part of her mind remained conscious. She heard distant moans and realized that she heard herself moaning in pain and lust. Then came a horrible roar from somewhere close by, and she saw one of the shadows moving.

The bear creature had returned, and now, in the center of the faces of its human victims was the horrified face of Eric. She saw him looking at her with shock and revulsion. For some reason, him watching her being fucked by this hidden creature made her cumming even more powerful.

The bear creature wandered off, taking the human faces with it. The cock tentacle, or whatever you would call it, swelled itself to a girth that threatened to split her in two.

The head of the cock was so large that it could never have been withdrawn from her cunt, but that idea obviously was never part of the plan. When she thought that she could no longer accommodate any more growth of the thing, she felt a strong pulsing in its tissue, and so much cum spurted from the creature that her stomach actually distended to find room for the semen.

Through the haze of her orgasmic ecstasy, she noted in some alarm that it did not diminish and withdraw from her. Indeed, it began to return to the rhythmic movement of fucking her again.

It was the third, or perhaps the fourth, time that it came in her that the power in the lantern finally gave out, and the cave was plunged into total darkness.

By this time, Rebecca didn't care anymore. The last of her mind had spun away into oblivion, and the only sensation that remained to her was an insatiable lust for the fucking of the beast. As long as she lived, this would be her life.

THE END

ABOUT THE AUTHOR

SE BLOOM IS AN AMERICAN Author of romance novels with historical or para-historical, paranormal, and erotic elements. She was born and raised in the Deep South and is currently living in the quaint little college town of Magnolia, Arkansas with two dogs, one daughter, and a devoted husband. She is exactly where she wants to be.

If you wish to contact the Author for any appropriate reason, you may email her at sheilaebloom@gmail.com.

ALSO BY SE BLOOM

THE SECRET BLOODLINE[1]

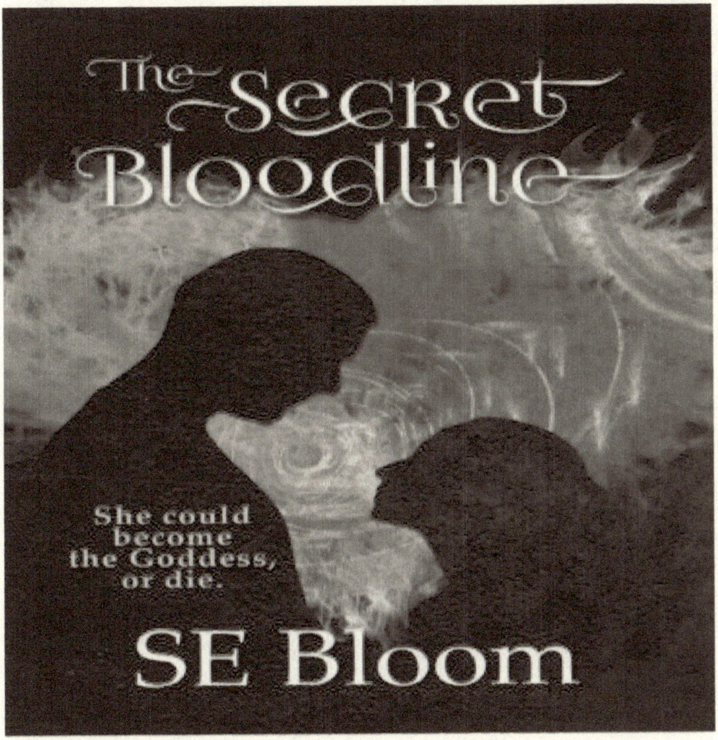

A description and excerpt from this book follows:

1. https://books2read.com/u/3J8p1J

DESCRIPTION OF
THE SECRET BLOODLINE

A WORLD THAT OPERATES in the shadows has set its sights on Dolma, a seemingly normal young woman living a routine life.

Dolma first encounters the alluring Lucas in a sensual dream.

Later he reveals himself in her real life, telling her she is in danger. Two opposing factions in the immortal world want her to join them, and each is determined to kill her if she makes the wrong move.

Lucas claims he can help her and warns they must flee from those hunting her. He assures her that's he's the person who can teach her to tap her own immense powers.

On the run from those who belong to the two bloodlines of the gods, Dolma finds Lucas irresistible physically but wonders how much she should trust this attractive and mysterious stranger.

If you enjoyed this book, you might also enjoy this following excerpt from THE SECRET BLOODLINE.

1 DREAM LOVER

"WHERE THE HELL AM I?" Dolma asked herself. There was cold gusting wind in this place. The wind found no resistance in the flimsy light green and see-through nightgown in which she found herself. She shivered and pulled the wispy garment tighter against the goose bumps that covered her skin.

It was darker than dark in this windswept and wooded land. The moon showed an outline of light in the heavens, obscured as it was by dark and angry clouds. The light that the moon provided served only to amplify the darkness of the night, and the shadows that the light from the moon cast.

There were deep and guttural sounds deep in the cover of the trees and underbrush of the woods. The sounds struck at Dolma's nerves and screamed that predators were near. At any moment, they would come out of the darkness.

There was a strong smell in the air, which she could not identify. Her primitive mind insisted that it was the smell of a nearby hunting predator. Her mind envisioned the smell as being the harbinger of a big cat. It could be a leopard or even a tiger.

She felt completely vulnerable. She was out in unknown woods, which could be miles from the nearest human help. She was almost naked, with only a barely-there gown to protect her from the elements. She did not even have on a bra or panties, not to speak of shoes! As soft and silky as the garment was, it still hardened her already rigid nipples as it moved over them.

Suddenly, in a moment where the wind died down, all the noises in the thickets fell silent. The odor of the unseen predator became intense, and only a single growling note sounded from nearby.

As cold as she was, Dolma felt a faint bead of sweat form on her brow, generated by the fear that was rising like a tide. She was feeling almost suffocated by the smell of that thing in the brush, and instant-by-instant, she was losing all control of her body. Soon, she would be a mindless animal, running from the tiger.

A loud and sudden roar sounded near-by, and she bolted in the opposite direction from the way it had come. She heard movement in the brush behind her. She felt the slashing heat that came from forcing her body through the briars and vines that obstructed her way to that possible haven in the other direction.

She expected to feel claws in her back and neck within seconds of her headlong flight, but the sounds of pursuit stayed behind her, further than could be credited to her running speed. The thing must be playing with her, like a cat with a helpless mouse.

She saw a slight opening ahead, with a little more moonlight, and an end to the tree cover for a span. If she could make it to there, perhaps the predator might not pursue her, if it was not too hungry, or in too playful a mood. It did not look like the sort of place that an ambush predator would enjoy.

She cleared the last hurdle of vines and sprinted for the last tree and the freedom that lay beyond it. The noise behind her sounded closer for a second, and then, she became so involved with her bid for life that she lost track of where it was located.

Dolma's headlong flight ended abruptly with a collision with a tall, darker figure, which had been standing on the other side of the last tree. When she hit his hard, lean body, she lost her balance and almost fell.

Dolma heard the strangest thing, a thing she could not quite pin down. She heard the whisper of a man's voice, a whisper that sounded like it came from far away, and as though it came from the figure in front of her.

The stranger grabbed her around her waist and cupped her ass with one hand to keep her upright. She regained her balance, but he seemed to have no intention of letting go of her.

As she struggled to release herself from her prison of arms, she looked frantically behind her. She had to assure herself that claws and teeth were not closing on her from the shadows. She no longer heard or saw any indication of her pursuer.

"Hey, there, sexy," the man said, "Where are you going in such a hurry?"

She struggled briefly to free herself before she replied. "There was something back there! We need to get out of here!"

The small voice was still there, and now it was whispering that she wanted the man, that no other person in the world was more important to her. Not all of her shivering was coming from the cold and the fear anymore. A tiny seed of moist need was blooming in her body.

She heard a chuckle. "I think that we are okay. I should thank whoever, or whatever brought me such interesting company."

The man increased his attention to the feeling of her exposed and vulnerable skin. Despite her best efforts to recover, the roaming hands were having the effect of making her nipples even more rigid, and she felt her core becoming wetter by the second.

The man's deep blue eyes and the darkness that his brown mane lent to his look were becoming a lure to everything inside of her that wanted a man. This wasn't the way she was supposed to be feeling!

"Stop it!" she commanded. The man was feeling like more of a predator than whatever that thing was that she had been fleeing. She wanted him to stop, and let her go.

Of course, she did. She was an independent woman, and none of this should be happening without her permission. So why was her body responding to his touch, instead of recoiling from his invasion of her self-determination?

He was delivering hard kisses to her neck and her mouth, forcing his tongue into her mouth, and the force with which he sucked at her neck would likely produce the bruising of a hickey. It was as though he felt that he owned her now.

Despite herself, a moan of desire escaped her when he began to massage her pussy through the thin fabric that protected it. He held her body in an open position, bowed slightly backward, to make her front entirely accessible.

He reached down, lifted the hem of the garment, and worked his hand up and into her pussy, where he began to work his will upon her body. The sensations were so overwhelming that she started to buck and orgasm as soon as his hand made contact with her sensitive core.

Her control was gone. She bucked her pussy into his grasp, as wave after wave of orgasms passed through her body. She wanted him to stop. She wanted him to go on forever, and never stop touching her skin. She wanted to be his toy, to do with as he willed. This wasn't her!

Orgasm after orgasm shook her, and each one took a part of her mind away until she was becoming a mindless fucking machine. If this stranger could make her feel this, without even having his cock, what could he make her feel with a proper fuck?

Finally, a last orgasm took the remaining bit of her consciousness away, and she opened her eyes, to find herself secure, at home and in her own bed. Her panties were soaked from desire, her nipples were hard and sensitive, and even the touch of the sheets on her skin threatened to start the uncontrolled sequence of orgasms all over again.

Angela is lying beside her in the bed. She snuggled close to Dolma, and gave her a passionate kiss on the mouth, as she touched Dolma's small breast with her glowing black hand. Dolma felt a kind of orgasmic aftershock from the soft touch.

"Baby, you want some pancakes?" Angela asked. "It looked like you had a good dream. Maybe we can recreate the dream later?"

"It wasn't that great a dream," Dolma denied. "Pancakes sound good. Pretty please, will you make me some?"

"You got it, baby," Angela smiled. She got out of the bed and began to saunter naked toward the kitchen. Dolma smiled as she noted mentally for the hundredth time that Angela thought herself far more irresistible than was the actual case.

Not that Angela was not a very attractive girl. She was the spitting image of Lisa Bonet at her best. Both Angela and Dolma were in their prime, both were twenty-four years old. Both had matriculated at the same college, where they had been roommates and friends.

Neither of the girls was gay, but they had fallen into the habit of having occasional sex when the need for a soft touch was caused by a harsh world. Dolma had always been the mousy one. Angela was one of those girls that consistently displayed that confidence in her sexuality that every woman aspires to feel.

They had fallen into this consoling sexual activity in the last two years. This sporadic thing had begun as an attempt to make the more repressed Dolma feel better after events that had left her feeling like a failure. It started with Angela trying to help her friend, but lately, it had been Angela who seemed to seek it out. She was beginning to become a clingy stranger to Dolma.

One of the Author Sheila E Bloom's favorite recent reads is a book called 'Beyond the Chaos Gate,' written by Quentin Ravensbane. It is a Lovecraftian Horror novel, and it supplies both horror and food for thought.

Here is an excerpt of that book here for you to enjoy, conveniently located on the next page.

10 OLD ONES

GARRET, JONNY, AND Oscar had just finished their first big carafe of beer and was working on the second one when Wilber finally graced them with his presence. Traveling in his wake was a smallish, bespeckled and bookish appearing man.

Thursday 11, 2019 @ 6:30 PM

"Hey, everybody, I would like you to meet Ira Stone," Wilber introduced. "Ira is an Occult Historian, which is a fancy way of saying he knows about occult practices of the past."

"Happy to meet you, Mr. Stone," Oscar said. "Maybe you can shed some light on what is happening. At this point, the supernatural is an acceptable explanation."

"That would be Dr. Stone," Ira corrected, "and yes, I have some ideas that might explain what is happening here and around the world."

"If you guarantee that you will keep what we tell you confidentially," Garret began, "we will give you the unabridged version of events, in exchange for your best insights into what is going on."

Garret went on to fill Ira in on the odd natures of the murder scenes, and the general degeneration of the town's inhabitants. He even mentioned the octopus substitutions and the fungus, concluding that they would be required information for any informed interpretation of events.

"Between what the murder scenes contained, and the odd dream that we all have every night," Ian explained, "and how things are going downhill, we think that the killers are trying to bring Yog-Sothoth into our world."

"That might be hard," Jonny added, "considering that this Yog-Sothoth is fictitious."

"Don't be too sure that the Old Ones are fiction," Ira corrected. "Although H.P. wrote about them as fiction, the idea of them, or something like them, is a long-standing Archetype of our species."

"You are saying that the demonic entities are real?" Ian asked, "even though Lovecraft didn't know that they were real?"

"That about sums it up," Ira admitted. "The thing is, we don't really just know about the past. We also know about things that are happening now but far away, and we know about things that will happen sometime in the future, in some dark little corner of our minds.

You see, time is really not a linear thing. If you believe in parallel universes, then even identifying *which* timeline past is *your* past is difficult. You can't know a future event as an event in your absolute future because every event splits the worldlines into two or more possible worldlines. Which version of your future self will experience that future event? If the worldline splits, each of the worldlines will have a version of you. Are they both you?

The past and the future are not as certain as we believe. There are future events that are of much higher probability than others as the future outcome of most past worldlines along the same branch of parallel universes.

If one of these probable event outcomes in a future timeline is supremely dangerous, fearsome, or just plain terrifying, then that future event could traumatize the past. If you remember the miniseries CHILDHOOD'S END, the alien caretakers were linked to the end of the species, and so, their appearance was seen as the face of evil, and their form became the standard form of the devil.

Now, imagine that an even greater and fearsome entity arrives here that has the ability to change the very fabric of reality. This trauma could be translated back through eons, and manifest itself as a sort of shadow, or weaker doppelganger, of the original future entity."

"You are saying that Yog-Sothoth could be a real entity from the future," Oscar exclaimed, "and that there were actual creatures that were 'dimmer' versions of Yog-Sothoth that existed in the deep past here on Earth."

"That is correct," Ira said. "My best guess is that they would have manifested during the Ediacaran period on Earth, from about 635 to 541 million years ago. I suspect that the Old Ones, even though they were just a manifestation of a future entity, still forced the fabric of reality to change and to force certain types of changes to the organisms on Earth.

Whenever they appeared, they persisted until sometime in the early Cambrian era. During the later Ediacaran and the early Cambrian, the phylum of Mollusks appeared, and the cephalopods were one branch of them. We all know the qualities of snails and Octopi, but what you might not know is that they are the branch of life forms that are distinguished as the only Earthly organisms that use copper as the transporter of oxygen in their blood instead of iron.

At any rate, the Old Ones were probably responsible for the origin of multi-cellular animal life on Earth, including the Cephalopods. In theory, true plants existed before the Ediacaran, but there was significant advancement during the period.

Before they appeared, the life forms on this planet were 'sort of plants' and bacteria, and while they were here, the animal-like organisms which were probably not animals or plants, but something in between, became primitive animals. In short order, they exploded into thousands of species.

If we take what Lovecraft wrote as true, then we have some alien colonists here on Earth to thank for restraining the Old Ones from holding the planet in an iron tentacle for all eternity. Even though the Old Ones were a pale copy of the future intruder, still they would not have allowed humans to become dominant on the planet if they were around.

I think that Lovecraft was reporting more of the truth than he realized. I believe that Sitchin's conclusion that the Anunnaki were aliens that ruled the prehistoric world of man is also true and may be a similar sort of future event reflection, or it may have just been a past event.

So, yes, I think that the Lurker at the Gate that you all feel is actually real, and threatens our world. These creatures are spreaders of chaos and madness, so assume those qualities will get worse and worse in the world, until either the beast is defeated, or he defeats us."

Ian felt both validated, and alarmed, by the direction in which the conversation seemed to be heading. If you read between the lines, it did not sound like they had much of a chance.

The conversation continued for a good long while, during which time the group went through a significant quantity of beer. Along about 11:15 PM, Wilber and Ira prepared to go to the station to do the show.

Wilber and Ira had both agreed more than once to conduct the conversation in such a way that the audience would be well informed, in case they believed it, and it made any difference. They also agreed not to divulge any of the information pertinent to the cases. Garret was not entirely confident that they would keep their word, but at this late date, it probably did not matter.

Shortly after the talk-show participants left the bar, the rest of the group decided to call it a night as well. Since they had no other customers left in the bar, Freya decided that she could close the bar down early, and then she would continue her budding romance with Ian, by spending as much of every day as she could around him. She definitely planned to go home with him again tonight.

By 11:30, the unmotorized individuals had caught rides with the motorized people, and all were headed home.

11 TIME, LOVE, AND DARKNESS

I DREAM OF A SHALLOW sea of gray waters and matted green moss-like plants in the tranquil surf and hugging the rocky beach tightly. The air is fetid with the smells of rich decay, that odor that speaks of short-lived generations of life.

Protruding from the foaming waters are the reddened summits of stromatolites, doing their part to pump life-giving and life-destroying oxygen into the air. Crab formed creatures scuttle in the shallow waters, and here and there insect formed things pick their way to unknown destinations. Of the things that crawl and swim within the seas, the most familiar are the trilobites.

The land is barren, for the world is yet millions of years too young for land-dwelling animals to develop. It has only been a handful of megayears since the first true animals separated themselves from things that were not yet animals. The dry lands are all rocks and dust formed by the first lichens leaching nutrients from the face of the stones.

Beyond the Stromatolites, some structures soar above the waters. In the shallow seas are gleaming black towers of obsidian that stand at least a thousand feet tall, like primeval archetypes of mortal attempts to reach the gods.

Once these must have been the bustling center of a great metropolis, but now, all is silence. A tendril of curiosity pulls me at great speed into the nearest of these towers.

The black walls of gleaming stone are covered in places with thick layers of primitive algae, and some ancient fungi lived upon the green remains. Nowhere can I see any sign of habitation, but only the despair of the tomb.

All is dead within these walls, but even the dead leave traces, the screams of pain, the sense of loss, all of these things endure after death. They have soaked into the stones of this place, and the voices of the dead are deafening.

I understand that once a species lived in these towers that sought to learn all things and to ascend to a greater existence beyond the mortal coil. I feel without seeing that some Thing reached down from another place, and touched these noble people with the rotting touch of decay and madness. The mere touch of this dark power made animals of this great species and created great things of nightmare to consume the last morsels of their essence.

The despair and the pain overwhelm me, even though they are but the smallest echo of that remembered time only half a gigayear ago. They overwhelm me, and I feel myself becoming unmade before the darkness rises up and takes me, and I know no more.

Friday 12, 2019 @ 7:30 AM

IAN OPENED HIS EYES and found that he was secure in bed at home, with the sleeping form of Freya at his side. He felt a smile crack his face, as he thought how lucky he was, even in the face of this unknown horror that he knew was drawing near.

He took a moment to breathe the scent of her perfume in deep, before he slipped out from under the bed sheets, and padded to the kitchen to start a breakfast for them. This time, she could take it easy while he burned the bacon.

He decided to cook bacon and skip the eggs, going straight to making a plate of pancakes. He mixed the batter and cooked the bacon. He griddled the pancakes with butter, using an iron skillet. He had just completed the task when Freya breezed into the kitchen, like a breath of fresh air.

She gave him a peck on the lips. She also gave him that 'hurry up and serve' look that only loved ones and puppy dogs can muster.

"Looking good," she said as she poured herself a cup of coffee. "There is nothing like a good sleep to give a girl an appetite." She smiled as she sat down at the breakfast table.

"How do you feel about company today?" Ian asked. "I am getting used to having you around."

"Yeah, but isn't that having you around me?" Freya protested with a smile. "I demand my full measure of protection and adoration!"

"It is all yours," Ian agreed amicably. "The only good things about our current apocalypse are that I get to hang around you, and everyone is effectively on vacation until this all blows over."

"Here is hoping," she replied, apparently referring to the 'blowing over' part. "We should probably walk to the bar right after we finish eating."

They didn't go to the bar immediately after eating. They actually had another cup of coffee each before taking a walk through the drizzling rain and the foggy landscape. Nevertheless, by 9:30 AM, they were ready to depart for the Starlight's End.

Ian found two umbrellas that he had stashed and forgotten about a long time ago. He gave one of them to Freya, and he braced himself to use his as a shield against the elements.

When they left his cottage, they entered another world, a dreary place that had somehow replaced the world of green plants and blue skies that the pair of them were starting to miss more than they would admit. There were sounds behind the fog, sounds that may have had a natural origin, but somehow, even the familiar became strange in this place.

Freya started walking close by Ian's right shoulder, making contact with him at every unexpected sound. Ian felt both flattered and worried about her need for his protection. He wanted her to need and want him, but he evaluated his ability to defend another as at the level of a defiant Chihuahua.

Ian could only see about ten feet through the fog. There was a strange, low-frequency sound coming out of the obscured areas ahead of them. Freya made another contact with his side, and then she grasped his hand ferociously.

As best they could, they navigated their way in the proper direction, using the sidewalk and other indicators of the correct direction to go. They came to the beginnings of the town park, a shortcut across which would shorten their journey considerably.

As they stepped onto the short mowed grass of the park, a strange smell suddenly came to their attention. It was not as pungent as a corpse, but it was a vaguely foul smell, which fit in well with the obscuring fog.

They only had to go a few feet to the first trees. The park was full of Oaks, and Cedars, and a few Hickory trees, such as the first tree they encountered. There was a sudden sharp rise in the unexplained noises, just as a large dead tree with crows on every barren branch reared up out of the fog.

The closer they got to the tree, the stronger and more pungent the odor that wafted up from it. The crows were raucously protesting their presence here at their private haven. The crows were glaring in a manner that struck Ian as a menacing manner, and he put a protective arm around Freya and steered a path clear of the tree and its crows.

Ian was starting secretly to fear that they had lost their way in the drizzle and mists when suddenly the Starlight's End loomed up out of the fog bank. It was with a sense of relief that the two of them stumbled into the bar, shutting the door between them and a world that was becoming increasingly alien.

Garret on the way to Oscar's Lab 10:00 AM

GARRET DROVE THE FLEET Impala that the precinct had loaned him to the South side of Holden, where the water plant, and Oscar's laboratory, was located. On the way to see Oscar, he caught a glimpse of a car tailing him, about two hundred feet behind his vehicle. He got just enough of a look at the car to be pretty sure that it was that of Detective Crawford.

He pulled into the parking lot and made his way into the facility. With the aid of a helpful Operator, he found the lab and knocked on the door. As he expected, Garret found Oscar busy conducting the daily water tests.

"I came by to check on your conclusions about the fungus among us," Garret said. "I think that Crawford followed me here, so keep your eyes open out in the world. I believe that his loyalties might be suspect."

"Yes, he has always seemed a little off," Oscar agreed, "and he has been getting more off by the day recently."

"Keep it under your hat," Garret instructed. "We don't want to provoke any negative reactions from him if we can help it."

Oscar agreed with that assessment of the situation since he was not by nature a very confrontational type of guy. "That fungus is some bizarre stuff," Oscar explained. "If there were another classification for organisms somewhere between fungi and animals, I would class it there. It is like nothing that I have ever heard of before."

"I don't have access to DNA analysis equipment, but I would be willing to bet that the fungus is not related to any other life forms on the planet," Oscar explained. "It is aggressive in a predatory way, and yet it also seems to be able to merge different organs together in a grafting process that I cannot explain.

It would appear to have been left at the murder scenes by someone, and it seems to be to merge the cephalopod and human bodies together. I suspect that if the fungus has enough time to work on the flesh, it may be able to bring it back into a semi-living state, in the sense that the corpse would be able to move around, and parts of the circulatory system would be functioning.

The reason I say that is because there were a few human cells trapped on the hyphae of the sample you gave me, and in a matter of hours, they changed from very dead to some weird sort of inactive state with a functioning cell metabolism. I have no doubt that they would become active-but-changed cells if they were given a few more hours for the change."

"Things have really gotten crazy around here," Garret complained. "Give me a plain old killer any day, but they can keep this zombie shit."

Oscar pulled out a file folder containing everything that he had found in the investigation of the fungus. Garret noted with interest that Oscar had conducted several tests on chemical vulnerabilities of the fungus to various poisons. It was also a little depressing that, overall, the fungus was not nearly as vulnerable as your typical organism.

Garret added the folder to other files in his briefcase dealing with other aspects of the cases. He decided that it was probably time to visit the local library to see if he could discern the commonalities of the crimes that might suggest a course of action.

Garret went down into the parking area and got into his car. He was actually looking forward to spending an hour or two at the library. The library itself was a relatively extensive facility for such a small town, and Garret looked forward to the peace and quiet.

Garret had always had an eye for finding patterns in activities and objects, which was one of the reasons he had gravitated to investigative work. A nice quiet space with nobody bothering him promised to advance his understanding of the patterns in this case.

As Garret made the left turn out of the parking lot, he saw Crawford's car parked in the street in the other direction for just an instant, before the turn hid the car from his view once again. *'I see that he hasn't given up yet,'* Garret thought. That situation is one that that would be best handled later.

Oscar's lunch at 12 PM

OSCAR FOUND A TEMPORARY stopping point in the lab testing regimen, for once in a timely manner for taking a meal on the official schedule. He decided that he would grab a burger at the Dairy Diner, the only full-fledged eating establishment in town.

He pulled into the parking for the cafe, got out and went in to get his burger, and maybe play one or two games of pool on the only public pool table in town. He encountered the trim, brunette waitress named Gail when he got inside and ordered his food.

While she filled his order, he racked up the balls for a game of pool. He had intended just to do a practice game, but one of the other customers came over and laid down his quarters on the table. The challenge was on!

It was nearly one in the afternoon when he had finished his burger, and trounced the other guy a couple of times at pool. He decided that it was time to head back, and left the cafe, started his car, and began the short journey back to the lab.

When he pulled into the parking space, he noticed that something was wrong. An emergency exit door opened into the parking area from the back of the lab. It was usually shut and barred, but now it was ajar. The alarm on the door was disarmed long ago, but it should not be open.

Oscar went through the door, to encounter a mess that wasn't present when he left for lunch. It was evident that someone had gone thoroughly through every place in the lab where something might be hidden, and he noticed immediately that the sample of fungus was gone.

Someone had obviously broken into the lab and tossed the place, and the target was evidently the fungus sample. It was time to call Garret and let him know what was going on.

A few moments after he called Garret, the Special Agent pulled up beside the door. Getting out of his car, he verified that the door had indeed been forced, and then he entered and had Oscar fill him in on his experience.

Garret took notes for a few minutes until the well of information ran dry, and then he put his pad and pen away. "I think that Detective Crawford may have done this," Garret said. "He was tailing me when I came to visit you earlier. I am almost sure that the man is *not* on our side anymore."

"I think this town is full of people that are no longer on our side," Oscar suggested. "I think that whatever is happening here is affecting most of the individuals in this town's minds.

Given the likely uselessness of reporting this crime to the same precinct which hosted the probable culprit, the two men mutually agreed not to make an official report. Besides, the fungus had already yielded most of the secrets that it was likely to produce, so no real harm was done.

The two of them hung around the lab for almost another hour, before Oscar decided that he was done for the day. By mutual consent, they agreed that they would stop at the bar for a little while, and have a few cups of coffee as they discussed the general situation with each other, and whoever of the other group members were present.

Friday, April 12, 2019 @ 3:20 PM

GARRET AND OSCAR HAD just arrived at the Starlight's End and managed to procure a cup of coffee for themselves when the door opened, and Jonny and Wilber came in. This made the gathering complete, even if nobody had called a meeting.

There were no other customers in the place, just the six of them, including Freya. Having no reason to maintain the watchful diligence of the waitress, she brought a carafe of coffee to the table and sat down.

"It is getting dangerous out there," Garret cautioned. "Oscar here had his lab broken into and items missing. People are changing for the worse, and more and more of them are apparently developing evil intentions. I don't know why we are as resistant to what is happening as we are, but it will probably mark us as their enemies at some point, so we must be careful."

"Are you ready to accept that something unworldly is happening here, Garret?" Ian asked. "I know that it is a hard thing to take for you, but I don't think that you can explain the changes in the people and the town, the murders, the fungus, or the dreams as normal things."

"I cannot explain the changes or the dreams, but they could still be caused by natural processes," Garret began, "and the murders could still be the acts of a deranged mind. Even the psychic power that you claim to possess could be nothing more than acute observation, and a subconscious mind that is good at seeing patterns and solving problems."

Wilber said, "Maybe so, but you must admit that to address a problem, you don't need to find the correct solution, just a solution that brings you the results you want. I assume that we want to resolve this problem with us winning, right?"

"You are right about that," Garret admitted. "We need to act as though the situation is dangerous and supernatural, and that we can defeat it by beating the people doing the bad things. If we find a more secure base to operate out of and assume that a win is possible, then we will be in the best shape that we can manage."

"There is plenty of room at my parent's house," Freya suggested. "It is a big house, and I worry that they are all alone there. They would be glad of the company.

Garret looked around at the other four people and discerned from their expressions that they were all okay with the change of venue. It stood to reason that Ian would go with whatever Freya wanted, and Oscar could use some security to calm his rattled nerves from the break-in. Wilber and Jonny would be happy to have a situation that delivered them a captive audience. It was settled, then.

"Okay, then," Garret said. "If you will make the arrangements with your parents, I will make a quick run in the morning to Tyler to get some provisions that we will need. We will need to develop an SOP for dealing with the current problem, and act to stop this stuff from happening."

Garret looked around the table once more, just to see if there was any dissension in the ranks. Everyone appeared to be on board with the plan, so he concluded that it was a done deal.

Freya was startled into almost rising to reassume her waitress role when the bar door opened and a man came in. It was Winston, in another of his rare visits to the bar he owned.

"Freya, this town is getting really dangerous out there," Winston said. "I no longer feel like it is safe to open the bar, even in the daytime, so I have decided that we need to close the bar for a while. I will pay you a base salary for the time we are closed, and we will open back up when this is over."

"What are you going to do, Winston," Freya asked in her cuddle-voice. "Is it safe around your neighborhood?"

"It is about the same as here," Winston admitted, "but I have a house in Dallas that I plan on moving into for the duration. It should be better than here."

"Adopt me," Jonny quipped. "Well, somebody has to say it."

For about 45 minutes the six and Winston had an energetic conversation that did not end with the adoption of Jonny, and it was agreed that the bar would close this afternoon, Winston would move to Dallas, and the six of them would all move into the house of Freya's parents.

With all of the important points addressed, Garret played taxi for Ian and Freya, taking them to his cottage, where Freya would call her parents, and arrange for tomorrows move.

Oscar also drove Jonny home, before driving to his own Spartan residence. He reflected that tomorrow would bring healthy changes, as well as a few bad ones.

If you enjoyed this book, please consider leaving an honest and positive review at the site where you purchased it. Your opinion and review are vital for the success of the Author in the cutthroat world of publication, and your review is also a prime way for shopping readers to determine whether the book is the book they want to read next.

Also by SE Bloom

The Secret Bloodline
Taken By The Slithering Horror